ماريك وأليسْ وعيد الميلاد

Marek and Alice's Christmas

Jolanta Starek-Corile
Illustrated by Priscilla Lamont

Arabic translation by Wafa' Tarnowska

"أسرعي يا أليسْ!" صاحَ ماريك.

"إنتظرْ دقيقةً، فإنني الفُّ هديّتَكَ!" صاحتْ أليسْ ردّاً عَليه.

"هلْ يمكنني أن أرى؟" سألَ ماريك آملاً أنْ تكونَ الهديّة درّاجة ناريّة ذاتَ أربعةِ دواليب.

"لا تكن سخيفاً،" أجابت أليسْ، "لا يمكنك رؤية شيء إلا بعدَ العشاءِ."

"حسناً، حسناً، أسْرعي! إنني ذاهبٌ لألْعَب،" قالَ ماريك.

"Hurry up Alice!" called Marek.

"Just a minute, I'm wrapping your present!" Alice shouted back.

"Can I see?" asked Marek, hoping it was a quad bike.

"Don't be silly, not until after supper," replied Alice.

"Ok, ok, but hurry up! I'm going out to play," said Marek.

عندَما خرجَتْ أليسْ، قذفَها ماريك بكُوَرٍ ثلجية. وحاولَ بوريس أن يُمسكَ بها.
"ظننت أنكما ستساعداني،" قالَ الجدُّ. "امسكا بالطرف الآخر لندخلَ الشجرة إلى البيت."
"هلْ أنتَ متأكدٌ أنَّ الشجرة كبيرة كفاية لتحمل كلَ هدايانا؟" سألَ ماريك.

When Alice came out, Marek threw snowballs at her. And Borys tried to catch them.
"I thought you were coming to help me," said dziadek. "Grab the other end and let's get this tree inside."
"Are you sure the tree is big enough for all our presents?" asked Marek.

"أعتقدُ أنَّ هذه الشجرة ممتازة،" أجابَ الجدّ.

"I think the tree is just right," replied dziadek.

عندما أُدْخِلَتْ الشجرة الى البيت بسلامة، إنتشرت رائحةُ الصنوبرِ في الغرفة.
ثم جاءَ البابا والماما بزينةِ الميلادِ وأخرجتْ أليسْ الملائكةَ وسلاسِلِ الورقِ
التي جلبتها من إنجلْترا من علبها.

Once the tree was safely inside, its fresh pine smell filled the room. Mum and
Dad came with the Christmas decorations, and Alice unpacked the little
angels and paper chains they'd brought from England.

في نفسِ الوقتِ أخذَ ماريك كل الشوكولا وعلَّقها كلَّها في مكانٍ واحدٍ.

"لا يمكنُكَ أن تفعلَ ذلك،" قالتْ أليسْ، "هذا سخيف."

"يمكنني أنْ أفعلَ ما أريدُ،" أجابَ ماريك، "لا أَستطيعُ أن أَصلَ أَعلى."

"هل تعلمين ما هو اجملُ شيئٍ في عيدَ الميلادَ البولوني؟ لا يجب علينا أن ننتظرَ حتى نهارَ العيدِ كي نفتَحَ هدايانا!" ثم ابتسَمَ ماريك فرحاً.

Meanwhile Marek took the chocolates and hung them all in one place.
"You can't do that, it looks stupid," said Alice.
"I can do what I like, and anyway I can't reach any higher," said Marek.
"You know what's so cool about Polish Christmas – we don't have to wait till Christmas Day to open our presents!" And he beamed with joy.

Just then the doorbell rang. It was Uncle Waldek with fresh carp for the supper.
Babcia was overjoyed. A visit from a man on Christmas Eve meant good luck.
"Are the fish still alive?" asked Marek. "I'm ready for fish and chips!"
"But you've just had breakfast," said Alice. "And you know that we have to fast
till supper."
But Marek wasn't listening. He was too busy playing with the fish.

ثم قرعَ جرسُ الباب. كان العمُّ قُالدك حاملاً سمكَ الكارْبِ الطازجِ للعشاء.

فرِحَتَ الجدَّةُ كثيراً لان زيارة رجُلٍ في ليلةِ عيدِ الميلادِ تُعتبَرُ حظاً سعيداً.

"هل مازالَ السمكُ حياً؟" سألَ ماريك. "إنني مستعدٌ لاكْلِ السمكِ مع البطاطاالمقليّة!"

"لكنَكَ قد انتهيتَ الآنِ من تناولِ الفطورِ،" قاَلَت أليسْ. "وأنَتَ تعْلَمُ أنكَ يجبُ أن

تصومَ حتى العشاءِ."

لكنَّ ماركَ لم يكُنْ يسمَعْ. كان مشغولاً يلَعبُ بالسمكِ.

"أتمنى لو كنت أستطيع اللعب معكما، لكن ما زال لدَيَّ الكثيرمن الطبخ،"
قالت الجدّة. ثم إنِّي أحتاجُ إلى مساعِدة.

"I wish I could play with you, but there's lots of cooking to do,
and I need some helpers," said babcia.

"سأساعدُكِ يا جدّتي," قالَت أليس، ثم وضعت مريلةً
وأخذت ملعقةً خشبيّةً لتحرّكَ مزيج بزرِ الخشخاش.
"ماريك، ألَن تساعد؟" نادت أليس.
"إنني لا أحبُّ الطبخَ، أحبُّ الأكْل!" أجابَ ماريك.

"I'll help," said Alice putting on an apron and taking the wooden spoon to stir the
poppy seed mixture. "Marek, aren't you going to help?" she called.
"I don't like cooking, I like eating!" replied Marek.

قرَعَ جرسُ البابَ مرّةً ثانية. كانت أمُّ الجدّةِ تحملُ حِزَمةً من القَشّ.

The doorbell rang again. It was prababcia with a bundle of hay.

"لماذا جلبت القشَّ؟" سألَ ماريك. "هلَ ستأكلُ الحيواناتُ معَنا؟"

ضحكت أمُّ الجدّة ثم أجابت: "نحنُ نضعُ القشَّ تحتَ الطاولةِ لنتذكّرَ أن يسوع ولِدَ في إصطبلٍ، على سريرٍ من القشِّ." ثم ضمّتْ ماريك الى صدرِها.

"Why have you brought hay?" asked Marek. "Are the animals coming to eat with us?" Prababcia laughed. "We put the hay under the table to remind us that Jesus was born in a stable, on a bed of hay," she said, giving Marek a hug.

"يا سلام، انظروا الى هذا الطعامِ كلّه! أتعتقدون
أنَّ الطاولةَ ستنكَسِرْ؟" سألَ ماريك.

"لا تقلَقْ، إنّها طاولةٌ قويّةٌ جدّاً،" أجابَت الجدّة.

"لماذا يوجدُ صحناً إضافياً؟" سألَتْ أليس، معتقدةً أن جدّتها لم
تعدِّ بشكل صحيح.

إبتسمَت الجدّةُ وقالت: "نحنُ دائماً نضعُ صحناً وكرسياً إضافياً.
وذلك لإستقبال كلِّ من لَيسَ لديَهِ مكانٍ يذهب اليه في ليلَةِ عيدِ الميلاد!"

"Wow, look at all that food! Do you think the table will break?" asked Marek.
"Don't worry, that's a very strong table," answered babcia.
"Why is there an extra plate?" asked Alice, thinking babcia hadn't counted right.
Babcia smiled. "We always put an extra plate and chair. It is to welcome anyone
who has nowhere to go on Christmas Eve!" she said.

في المساءِ المبِكر وصلَ ما تبقّى من أفراد العائِلةِ. سلّمَ الجميعُ على بعضهم البعض بقَولٍ: "ميلادٍ سعيد!" وعناق وقبلة.

In the early evening the rest of the family arrived.
"Happy Christmas!" Everyone greeted each other with a hug and a kiss.

"هل رأيتُم أولَّ نِجمَةٍ؟" سألَ أوليك.

"لا بعْدْ، إننا ما نزالُ نراقب،" أجابَ ماريك. "لكن **لماذا** نحنُ نراقب؟"

"إنّ النجمةَ كنجمةِ بيتَ لحمٍّ. إنها إشارةٌ لكَي نبدأ بالعشاء،" قالتْ أليس.

"أنِّي اراها!" صاحَ اوليك فجأةً ونظرَ الجميعُ الى أولِّ نِجمةٍ مشعَةٍ.

"Have you spotted the first star?" asked Olek.
"Not yet, we're still looking," answered Marek. "But WHY are we looking for it?"
"Well, it's like the star of Bethlehem. It's the sign for us to start our supper," said Alice.
"I see it!!" Olek suddenly shouted and they all looked out at the first bright star.

حانَ الآن وقتُ العشاءِ. أحضرت الجدةُ الخبزَ المباركَ ليتشارك فيهِ الجميع حين تقديمِ التهاني.

Now it was time for supper. Babcia brought in the blessed bread for everyone to share, while offering wishes.

"أتمنّى لو كانت لدَيّ درّاجة ناريّة بأربعة دواليب," قالَ ماريك لأمه.
"لا يجبُ أن نقولَ كلماتٍ كهذه," قالتَ الأمُّ بغضب. "يجبُ ان تقدّمَ أمنياتك
الطيّبة لشخْصٍ آخر، ثمَّ إننا لَسنا في دكّانِ ألعاب."
"ما كنتُ أفكّر بالالعاب," اجابَ ماريك. "اذا كَان الله عظيماً، لماذا لا يجلُب
لـي درّاجةً ناريّةً بأربعة دواليب؟"
"لأنَّ الحياة ليست هكذا!" أجابت الأم.

"I wish I could have a quad bike," said Marek to his mum.
"You are not supposed to say things like that," said Mum
crossly. "You offer wishes to another person, and anyway
we are not in a toy shop."
"I wasn't thinking of toys," replied Marek. "If God
is so great, why can't He bring me a quad bike?"
"Because it doesn't work like that!" said Mum.

ثمّ صلّى الجدُّ والجدّةُ صلاةً
وجلَسَ الجميع لِيأكُل.

Then babcia and dziadek said a prayer and everyone sat down to eat.

"لا تَنَسوا ان تتذوقوا كلَّ شَيءٍ،" قالت الجدّة. "كلّما تذوقتم صَحناً كلّما أغتَنَت حياتُكم وأمتلأت."

"ماذا يعني هذا؟" سألَ ماريك حائراً.

"يعني أنّه يمكِن أن تحصِل على درّاجتك النارية ذاتِ الدواليبِ الأربعة،" أجابتْ أليس.

"Now, don't forget to try everything," said babcia.
"The more dishes you try, the more rich and
plentiful your life will be."
"What does that mean?" asked Marek, confused.
"It means you might just get your quad bike,"
answered Alice.

After supper everyone gathered round to sing carols. Alice played *Silent Night* on her recorder while Marek sang in English.

"Why can't he sing in Polish?" asked Olek.

"Because he hasn't learnt it yet," answered Alice quickly.

بعدَ العشاءِ إجتمعَ الجميع لترتيلِ تراتيلِ الميلاد. عزفت أليس أغنية
"ليلةَ ساكنةَ" على الناي بينما غنّى ماريك بالإنكليزية.
"لماذا لا يستطيعُ الغناءِ بالبولونية؟" سألَ أوليك.
"لأنه لم يتعلّمْها بعْد،" أجابت أليس بسرعة.

"هل يمكننا فتَحَ الهدايا قبلَ الذهابِ إلى قدّاسِ نصف الليلِ؟" سألت أليس.

"اريد فتحها الآن!" قال ماريك، دون ان ينتبه أنَّ الجدّة كانَت قد أعطت أولَّ هديّةٍ لأليس.

"يا سلامْ، كنتُ دائماً أريدُ فستاناً كهذا!" قالت أليس. "شكراً يا جدّتي!" ثمَّ عانقت جدّتها.

"Can we open our presents, before we go to Midnight Mass?" asked Alice.
"I want to open them now!" said Marek, but he hadn't seen that babcia had already given the first present to Alice.
"Wow, I've always wanted a dress like this!" said Alice. "Thank you babcia!"
And she gave her a hug.

"هَلْ حصَلْتَ على درّاجتِك النارّية ذاتِ الدواليب الأربعة ؟" سألَ أوليك.

"لا بَعْدْ،" أجابَ ماريك، "مَعَ أنني تذوقت كلَّ صحنٍ تقريباً ..."

"وأنتَ يا اوليك؟" سألت أليس.

"آه، لقد حصَلْتُ على هدّيةٍ كبيرةٍ في يوم عيد القدّيس نيقولاوس،" أجابَ أوليك. "اليوم هو يوم الهدايا الصغيرة."

لم يصدّق ماريك أن هدايا العيد قد فاتته فقال: "في السنةِ القادِمة انا قادمٌ في اوائلِ كانونِ الأول لقضاء عيدِ الميلادِ كلّهِ هنا."

"Did you get your quad bike?" asked Olek.
"Not yet," answered Marek, "and I tried almost every dish…"
"What about you, Olek?" asked Alice.
"Oh, I got my big present at the beginning of December," he replied. "We get them on St. Nicolas' day, today it's only small ones."
Marek couldn't believe he'd missed out. "Next year I'm coming at the beginning of December for the whole of Christmas," he said.

"تعالوا جميعاً، حانَ وقتُ الذهابِ الى قداسِ منتصَفِ الليلِ،" قالت الجَدّة.

"هل يمكنني البقاءَ في البيتِ معَ والدتكِ يا جدّتي؟" سألت أليس.

"ألا تريدينَ الذهابَ معنا؟ إنّ السهر ممتع،" قالَ ماريك.

"Come on everyone, it's time to go to Midnight Mass," said babcia.
"Can I stay at home with prababcia?" asked Alice.
"Don't you want to come? It will be so cool to stay up late," said Marek.

"لا اريدُ النومَ،" أجابت اليس. "قالت لي جدّتي أنَّ عندَ منتصَفِ الليلِ تستطيعُ الحيواناتُ النظقَ. فهذه الليلةَ الوحيدة التي يمكنني أنْ أتكلّم بها مع كلبنا بوريس."

"I'm not going to bed," said Alice. "Babcia says that at midnight all the animals can talk. So tonight is my only chance to talk to Borys."

في منتصفِ الليلِ كان ماريك وأليس نائمانِ نوماً عميقاً.

At midnight Alice and Marek were fast asleep.

The Family

Marek

Alice

Dzadek

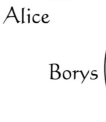

Borys

Babcia

Prababcia

Waldek   Olek

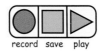

record save play

Christmas Cookies

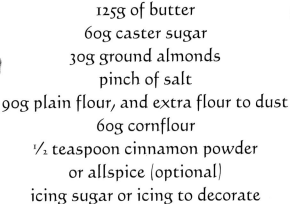

125g of butter
60g caster sugar
30g ground almonds
pinch of salt
90g plain flour, and extra flour to dust
60g cornflour
½ teaspoon cinnamon powder
or allspice (optional)
icing sugar or icing to decorate

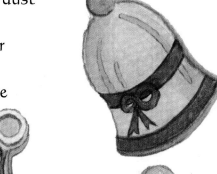

1) Beat the butter and sugar in a mixing bowl until fluffy

2) Then add the remaining ingredients and beat until the mixture sticks together and can be formed into a ball.

3) Dust a pastry board with flour and turn out the mixture. Then knead gently for a couple of minutes to form a smooth dough.

4) Next roll out the dough until it is about 5mm thick.

5) Choose some Christmas shaped biscuit cutters and cut into shapes.

6) Using a palette knife transfer the shapes to a greased baking sheet. Bake in a preheated oven (180°C/350°F/gas mark 4) for 15 minutes or until golden.

7) Leave to cool on the tray before lifting off. Decorate the shapes with icing sugar

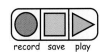

record save play

Advent Calendar

Touch the pictures and baubles to hear songs, information and activities.

record save play